School is done, I'm heading home.

It was such an awesome day!

I got the role of **NINJA MASTER**

in this year's school play!

How to Catch a MONSTER

From the New York Times
bestselling team

Adam Wallace &
Andy Elkerton

sourcebooks
wonderland

So now I'm feeling brave and strong,
and full of courage, too!
But if I'm going to be a **HERO**,
then there's one thing left to do!

How to be a NINJA

See, there's a MONSTER in my closet,
with claws and teeth and hair.
And tonight, I'm going to scare him!

He lives just right through there...

I spot my monster right away.
He's practicing his ROAR.
He almost scares me half to death,
but I won't be scared anymore!

I reach into my bag of tricks
and pull out my first trap.

I'll catch my monster right away.

It'll be a snap!

Okay, he's stronger than I thought.

But I'm not finished yet.

I'll catch him in my SUPER-STICKY

ninja-nabbing net!

Aack! He just ESCAPED again!
But my next trap will not miss.
I'll give him every trick I've got.
He won't get out of this!

I stare at him, and he stares back.
His monster eyes look sad.
"I'm sorry, friend. I really am.
Oh, please, just don't be mad."

"I never meant to scare you.

I did it by mistake.

It's hard to play when you're asleep.

I want you **wide awake!**"

So then I stop my NINJA BOT,

and he pulls the bars apart.

I shake his hand, and then he smiles...

"That's how we say hello, my friend.

We do it all the time!

Just take a whiff! You'll see it smells

like **strawberries** and **lime**."

And then he takes me to his house,

which seems a little weird.

He lets me meet his mom and dad.

Is this the **creature** that I feared?

We play for hours, and have such fun,

and eat Volcano Pie!

And when he throws me in the air,

he throws me really high!

Then, at last, it's time for bed.

He helps me brush my teeth.

But he squeezes all my toothpaste out...

he's strong beyond belief!

The night is done, and Mom comes in
to tuck me nice and tight.
I'm glad I'm feeling *safe and sound*.
It's time to say good night.

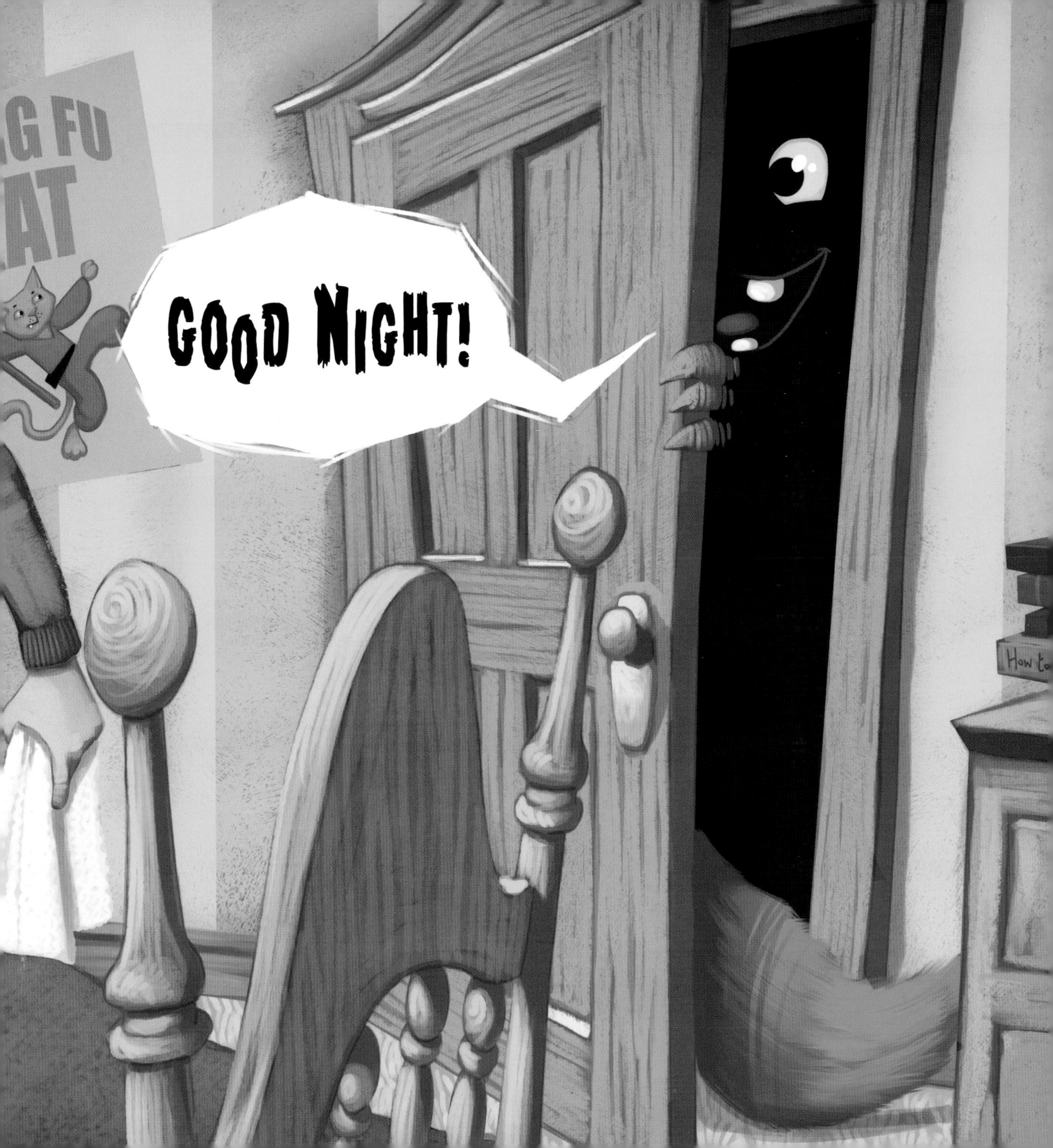
GOOD NIGHT!

Copyright © 2017, 2022 by Sourcebooks
Text by Adam Wallace
Illustrations by Andy Elkerton
Cover and internal design © 2017, 2022 by Sourcebooks

Sourcebooks and the colophon are registered trademarks of Sourcebooks.

The art was first sketched, then painted digitally with brushes designed by the artist.

The characters and events portrayed in this book are fictitious or are used fictitiously. Any similarity to real persons, living or dead, is purely coincidental and not intended by the author.

Published by Sourcebooks Wonderland, an imprint of Sourcebooks Kids
P.O. Box 4410, Naperville, Illinois 60567-4410
(630) 961-3900
sourcebookskids.com

Cataloging-in-Publication data is on file with the Library of Congress.

Source of Production: Worzalla, Stevens Point, Wisconsin, United States of America
Date of Production: July 2022
Run Number: 5024470

Printed and bound in the United States of America.
WOZ 10 9 8 7 6 5 4

CONNECT THE DOTS TO REVEAL A TRAP!

CAN YOU CATCH SIGHT OF THESE HIDDEN PICTURES?

 THE LETTER Q

FOUR HEARTS

A UNICORN HORN

THREE TOOTHPASTE TUBES

A KEY

A CROWN